I Wish I Was Big

tate publishing
CHILDREN'S DIVISION

Kelly Jean Lietaert

Published by Tate Publishing & Enterprises, LLC
127 E. Trade Center Terrace | Mustang, Oklahoma 73064 USA
1.888.361.9473 | www.tatepublishing.com

Tate Publishing is committed to excellence in the publishing industry. The company reflects the philosophy established by the founders, based on Psalm 68:11,
"The Lord gave the word and great was the company of those who published it."

Book design copyright © 2014 by Tate Publishing, LLC. All rights reserved.
Cover and interior design by Cecille Kaye Gumadan
Illustrations by Louise charm Pulvera

Published in the United States of America

ISBN: 978-1-63367-318-2
Juvenile Fiction / General
14.08.06

I Wish I Was Big

Kelly Jean Lietaert

To Steve, Joseph, Hannah, Elizabeth, and Mary Grace - You are my ♥

"I wish I was big," Lizzie mentioned as we read a book. "What would you do if you were big?" Mommy asked her.

Lizzie began talking fast, because she was anxious to share her ideas. "First of all, I'd use markers, not these silly old crayons." Mommy smiled and offered a suggestion. "If you are bored with your crayons, we could use chalk, paint, or even Play-doh."

"Well then, I'd stay up late, late, late—until the stars came out. Oh, and I won't take a nap or rest one little bit the whole day through!" "Yes," Mommy agreed, "staying up late is a special treat, but getting enough sleep at night will give you the energy to play the next day. Your body is growing, it needs downtime during the day to keep you healthy and strong."

With wide eyes and a dramatic twirl, Lizzie exclaimed, "I'd go to the movies and buy extra big popcorn and boxes of candy." Nodding, Mommy gently said, "Someday we'll take you to the theaters, but they can be very loud and sometimes little bottoms have trouble keeping the seats down. For now, let's enjoy watching videos cuddled on our bean bag chairs at home."

Not ready to give up quite yet, Lizzie continued. "I'd ride the cool yellow bus to school and stay the WHOLE day." "Oh, I absolutely agree that school will be wonderful," Mommy said, "but it's also quite fun to make our own schedule and have a good time together while the big kids are away."

Kicking her heels in the air, Lizzie declared, "I'd wear tall high heels just like you!" Mommy sighed, "High heels ARE fancy-schmancy, but your cozy bunny slippers are MUCH more comfortable and won't give your toes ouchies."

Now it was Lizzie's turn to sigh. "I'd go to my friend's house and play all day and then spend the night," she said, remembering how her older brother did this just the other day.

Mommy understood. "Yep. Playing at other people's homes is exciting, but so was sleeping downstairs in your sleeping bag, and the carpet picnics we have in front of the fire with our family."

"Sweet Lizzie, even though I think it's fun to look forward to the future, I also know that God wants us to be content with our lives right now. He has given us many blessings for us to appreciate today—not tomorrow. So, if you keep looking ahead, you will miss the exciting things in your life this very minute."

"Now," Mommy suggested, "how about we go and celebrate today by making some cookies?" "Sure," Lizzie agreed, "but only if I can lick the spoon!"

e|LIVE

---

listen|imagine|view|experience

AUDIO BOOK DOWNLOAD INCLUDED WITH THIS BOOK!

In your hands you hold a complete digital entertainment package. In addition to the paper version, you receive a free download of the audio version of this book. Simply use the code listed below when visiting our website. Once downloaded to your computer, you can listen to the book through your computer's speakers, burn it to an audio CD or save the file to your portable music device (such as Apple's popular iPod) and listen on the go!

How to get your free audio book digital download:

1. Visit www.tatepublishing.com and click on the e|LIVE logo on the home page.
2. Enter the following coupon code:
    b3ec-3492-5b58-8577-edf6-172d-20a3-f7a0
3. Download the audio book from your e|LIVE digital locker and begin enjoying your new digital entertainment package today!